FLIRTING
with my
BEST FRIEND

A FRIENDS TO LOVERS ROMANTIC COMEDY

GIA STEVENS

Flirting with My Best Friend: A Friends to Lovers Romantic Comedy by Gia Stevens

www.authorgiastevens.com

Published by: Gia Stevens

Editing by: My Notes In The Margin

Proofreading by: Illuminate Author Services

Print Edition

ISBN: 978-1-958286-01-2

For my husband.
Thanks for the extra push.

preface

Mark and Liana's story about takes place in the mid-2000's. Liana is the older sister of the hero in book one. After I wrote book one, I knew Liana needed a story about how she and Mark started dating. Enjoy!

Note to readers: While the story is a romantic comedy, one scene involves a sexual assault incident.

chapter one
I Bet You

Liana

"Cruz is going to hit a home run. I can sense it," I say to my best friend, Mark, before directing my attention back to the row of screens hanging on the wall behind the bar of The Sports Den. On the weekends, the employees move all the tables to create a large dance floor so all the college students can bump and grind on each other to Nelly, Outkast, and 50 Cent while drinking three-dollar pitchers of long island ice teas. Tonight's crowd is more low-key while they watch the game and order one of The Sports Den's famous burgers.

We watch most games from the comfort of one of our couches at our homes, but tonight's game is only airing on a premium paid channel, which is why we're watching from a barstool.

"No way. Rodriguez hasn't thrown a home run ball all season. He's not going to start tonight," Mark rebuts as he throws his hands towards the TV.

"He's doing it. Just wait." I sit up straighter on my stool.

"I bet you he doesn't. Loser buys the next round." Mark turns towards me; his gaze meets mine as he rests his forearm on the worn wooden bar top.

I hold out my hand, and when his large one envelops mine, we shake on it. "Deal. Might have to start drinking the fancy stuff next." I shimmy my shoulders, giving him a wink.

As Cruz takes the plate, both our eyes are glued to the screen. Rodriguez winds up and throws a curve ball across home plate.

"Strike one. Better get ready to buy me that drink." Mark pokes at my ribs.

I slap his hand away. "Slow your roll. It's not over yet."

Another pitch flies toward the plate. This time, Cruz's bat connects with the ball but unfortunately fouls into left field. *Come on Cruz,* I chant to myself. It's not about losing the bet. I'd buy Mark a beer anytime, but I just *can't* lose the bet.

Mark and I met our freshman year at Harbor Highlands College. We share a mutual love of baseball and Mark always reminds me it's the real reason we're friends. But I know deep down it was my wit and charm that drew him in. Soon after this budding friendship developed, we found enjoyment in trying to one-up each other by placing bets. We wager on everything from sports games to the weather. Both Mark and I played sports in high school, so being competitive came second nature. And neither of us liked to lose.

"Uh oh, it's not looking good."

"It's not over yet. One and one." My leg bounces on the barstool's foot ring.

Rodriguez launches a knuckle ball that flies into the glove of the catcher.

"Better get ready to pay up, Lee." Mark chuckles beside me.

I swat in his direction to shut him up, but he leans out of the way to avoid contact, his laughter becoming more prominent. My heart beats wildly in my chest as I tap the corner of the cardboard coaster on the bar top. Cruz steps up to the plate. I know that look in his eyes. He's got this one. Rodriguez releases the ball, and it's like time slows as the ball soars through the air. Suddenly, the bat connects with the ball. I hold my breath until the bar erupts with cheers as the ball lands somewhere in the upper deck. Within seconds I'm jumping out of my chair, cheering with the rest of the bar. I turn to Mark. "I do believe you owe me a drink." Mark just stares dumbfounded at the TV as if he's never seen a home run before.

"H-How did you know?"

I lean toward him. "Told you, gut feeling. You really should listen to me more often."

"Bullshit. I saw how nervous you were with the bouncing leg and all."

"A win's a win." I flash him a cheeky smile.

Mark glares at me from the corner of his eyes while he flags down the bartender to order another round. "And it's on him," I shout to her while pointing at Mark. "That was fun. Wasn't it?" I can't fight the smile on my face.

"It's only fun because you won. Next time you're going down."

"Bring. It. On."

The bartender tosses a couple of coasters on the bar and sets our beers on top. We grab them and tap the rim of our glasses together. Beer sloshes out and pools on the wood surface. We continue watching the game while heckling each other's favorite players.

Out of the blue, the bartender sets a pint of beer in front of me. "It's from the guy behind you." She lifts her chin in his direction.

I swirl around in my seat and sure enough, there's a table with three guys sitting behind us. The blond in the middle is staring right at me. I raise my glass to their table and mouth a *thank you.*

When I turn back around, Mark's eyebrows knit together. "How often do guys buy you drinks when you're out at the bar?"

"Sometimes." I shrug my shoulders and take a sip of my beer.

"Why don't girls buy me drinks?"

"Because I'm cuter than you are." I flash Mark a big, cheesy grin.

"Okay, okay, you got me there."

"But you're cute too," I tease as I reach over to pinch his cheek, but his arm shoots up to block mine.

"But seriously, why would they think it's appropriate to send a girl a drink who is clearly with a guy? What if I was your boyfriend?"

"Will this make you feel better?" I turn around to look back at the table of guys. I shove Mark in the shoulder while making a face like I just ate something disgusting. Turning back toward Mark I say, "There. That should clear that up."

Mark barks out a laugh. "Thanks for that."

We continue watching the game and chatting like we always do. Shortly after ten the game finally ends.

Mark releases a yawn. "Shit, I got class in the morning. I better get going."

"Yeah, I should probably get going too." I stand, my legs a little wobbly. While using the back of the stool to steady myself, I collect my phone and wallet from the bar.

"Let me give you a ride home. You don't have class until the afternoon, so I can give you a ride to pick up your car when I'm done with my morning class."

"That would be perfect. Thanks." We've hung out together so much that we know each other's sleep schedules, school schedules and eating schedules. Maybe our friends are right when they call us an old married couple? But that's what happens when two people spend all their time together.

Twenty minutes later, we're pulling up to the curb in front of the house I'm renting with three other girls. I open the door to Mark's Jeep and step out. Mark gets out and rounds the front to meet me on the passenger side to accompany me up the sideway. He's always been a gentleman, never letting me wander around campus in the dark or even the few hundred feet to my front door. When we reach the door, I turn towards Mark. The porch light casts a soft glow across his face.

"Fun night, as always." I rest my hands on his shoulders and stretch up on my tippy toes to place a kiss on his cheek. The light five o'clock shadow tickles my lips. His fingertips caress my bare skin as his hand grips my waist where my shirt has ridden up. The small touch sends a wave of goosebumps across my skin. Slowly, I pull away. His forest green eyes lock on mine, shifting back and forth, searching. His hand suddenly falls from my waist, and just like that, whatever little bubble we were just in bursts. "Chat with you tomorrow," I say, my voice soft.

He takes a step back. "Yeah, I'll call you when I'm out of class."

Mark turns and strolls down the sidewalk. My gaze lingers on his back before yelling, "Hey, Mark!" He pivots and with slow backward strides he stares back at me. "Saturday night. Party at the rugby house."

He waves his acknowledgement before turning back around. He climbs into his Jeep and I know he's going to wait until I go inside, so I give him a wave and open the front door. As I close it behind me, I lean my back against it and look up at the ceiling. That look was a look I've seen before but *never* from Mark and never directed at me.

chapter two
No Need to Complicate Shit with Feelings

Mark

Why did I say I would go to this party? Staying in and binge-watching *The Office* is more my speed. Plus, Sheila will be there and she has a hard time taking no for an answer. But in reality, the only reason I'm doing this is because of Liana. I have a hard time saying no to her. My phone buzzes in my pocket. Digging it out, I see it's a text.

Liana: Be there in 5.

After I respond, I flip the phone closed, tuck it back into my pocket, and wait for her outside.

"There are so many people here!" Liana shouts as "Get Low" by Lil Jon pumps through the speakers while rowdy college students hoot and holler at each other. "Let's find the keg." She takes my hand in hers, tugging me through the sea of people.

When we reach the back of the house, I hand over a ten-dollar bill to the guy next to the keg and in return, he passes us two red plastic cups. With our cups filled to the brim with cheap keg beer, we wander around the room waving to people we know and stopping to chat with others.

Liana finds a couple of girls from one of her classes and leaves me to go chat with them. My buddy Mason comes and stands next to me. "Man, you got it bad." He takes a drink of his beer.

I turn to look at him. "What are you talking about?"

"Liana. You just need to ask her out."

"She's my best friend. We don't need shit to get weird." My gaze drifts back to where she's talking animatedly with her friends.

"You watch her as she walks away. When she's gone, you look sad as hell. You're like a lost puppy whose owner just left for the day."

"You don't know what you're talking about." Taking another sip of my beer, I let his words sink in. Liana and I been friends since freshman year when we met at orientation. We have a great time together because we're friends and that's all. No need to complicate shit with feelings. That's how friendships are lost.

"Okay man. Whatever you say. But just know everyone sees it but you two. She's a great girl and you bet your ass some guy is going to come in and sweep her off her feet." He raises an eyebrow at me while he tilts his head.

Just then, Sheila saunters up to us. Too much makeup paints her face, while her shirt is about two sizes too small, cleavage spilling from the purposely ripped neckline, and shorts that I'm sure will show off her ass cheeks. Why she thinks this look is attractive is beyond me.

"Hey, Mark." Her sugary sweet voice leaves me with a toothache.

I give her a tight smile. "Hi, Sheila."

"Hey, Sheila," Mason says, but she just ignores him. He releases a laugh, knowing I have no interest in this girl but enjoying how uncomfortable she makes me.

She trails a finger over my chest as she purrs, "I didn't know you were going to be here."

Bullshit. She knows I'm friends with a few guys on the rugby team and she has seen me here on multiple occasions during one of their parties. "Yup. Here I am."

"Do you want to go somewhere and talk? I could really use your help in my Differential Equations class, and I know how smart you are in math."

"Um—" I try to think of a polite reason why I don't want to go anywhere with her, but luckily I don't have to because Liana comes to my rescue.

"There's beer pong. Come be my partner." Liana grabs my hand.

"Sorry, beer pong awaits," I say to Sheila while Liana tugs me toward the basement stairs where the beer pong table is set up.

Before we reach the crowd gathered around the table, I lean down and whisper to Liana. "May I say you have impeccable timing."

Liana calls the next game before turning to me. "Why's that?"

"Sheila wanted to go somewhere to talk about helping

her with a math class. But I have a feeling she wanted to calculate the amount of time it would take to get naked."

Liana lets out a laugh. "Oh, I should have let you sweat that out for a bit first."

"Our friendship might be over if you did."

We definitely underestimated our competition. I stare down at the opposite end of the table and see eight cups and then look down at our side with only three cups.

"Hey, beer pong queen. We better start making some cups, or we'll look like a couple of chumps."

She pats my chest. "We got this. You gotta toy with them a bit, make them think they're going to win, and then bam. They won't know what hit them. Watch this."

I chuckle. "If you say so."

Liana lines up her shot and throws the white ball down the table. The ball hits the rim of a cup and bounces to the floor.

I bend down to whisper into her ear. "Just like that, huh?"

"Shut up. Let's see what you got."

"I bet you breakfast tomorrow morning that I make this next shot."

"And if you miss, you owe me breakfast."

"Deal."

"What will I want for breakfast? A ham and cheese omelet sounds good. Oh, no waffles with strawberries. That sounds delicious."

"Yeah, it does. Sounds even better when you'll be making it for me." I line up my shot and throw. The ball lands directly into the top cup, beer splashing onto the table. "That ham and cheese omelet is going to taste so good."

"It's a bet worth losing since you've *finally* made a cup." She looks up and gives me a wide grin. I can't help my own smile. In the next round, both teams come up empty-handed. "What do you think? Time to run the table?"

"Let's do it."

Liana holds the ball up in the air and closes one eye, lining up for the perfect throw. The ball soars through the air and falls directly into a cup. I do the same and my ball falls into the cup next to hers. Liana jumps up and down and gives me a high five. "Bring 'em back!"

We both take our next turn, once again sinking both balls. Everyone in the basement is watching the game intensely, wondering will win.

"Re-rack!" Liana yells down the table and they make the triangle from the last three remaining cups. Liana throws her ball and makes another cup. But when I throw mine, the ball lands in the empty spot a cup once stood.

"That's alright. We're up two to three," Liana says, rubbing her hands together in front of her.

The two guys on the other end take their shots. One makes it, the other misses.

Liana rolls the ball between her hands and eyes the two cups on the other end. "I'll take the one on the left. You take the one on the right and let's end this."

This girl has all the confidence in the world, and I love that about her. Sometimes she gets it wrong, but she can easily push that aside and keep moving forward. She throws her ball and just like she said, it lands in the cup on the left. I follow suit, and my ball lands in the cup on the right. A loud cheer erupts from everyone watching the game. Liana turns to me and jumps into my arms, wrapping her legs around my waist. Completely surprised by her actions, I recover quickly and wrap my arm under her butt to hold her to me. She throws her hands up in the air and celebrates. As I let go, her body slowly slides down mine with my hand still resting on her lower back, my pinky resting on the spot right above the curve of her ass. Trying to keep all impure thoughts of my best friend out of my mind, I turn back toward the two guys at the end of the table, disbelief written all over their faces.

"You each get a rebuttal." I bounce both balls back to them. They make them both and we go back to three cups. If they miss, we win. Luckily, our premature celebration wasn't for nothing, as they both miss their shots. We continue to play and dominate in two more games until we've finally consumed our fair share of beer, to the point where six cups are looking more like twelve.

"Let's get you home. Remember, you owe me breakfast." I wrap my arm around Liana's shoulder as she wraps hers around my waist. Her other hand rests on my chest to help her balance. The gentle touch of her fingertips sends a rush of heat below my belt. *Not happening buddy.*

We walk back to her place and I help her up the porch steps to the front door. She fumbles with her keys a moment before the door opens. Stepping inside, she turns back to me. "You staying?"

This isn't the first time I've slept in the same bed as Liana. Sometimes one of us is too tired from studying or has one too many drinks to make it home. But something about tonight feels different. I push those feelings aside because this shouldn't be anything different. My gaze meets Liana's, and she quirks an eyebrow at me, silently asking if I'm staying or going. I nod, walking past her as she closes the door behind us.

In her room, Liana pulls back the covers of her queen-size bed. One perk of staying at her place is that she has the superior bed.

"So, Jess told me about some speed dating event the student activities board is hosting. They're trying to find fun and creative ways to get students together. Wanna go?"

I toe off my shoes as I undo the button on my jeans. "Speed dating? People still do that?"

Liana opens her dresser drawer and retrieves a pair of pajamas. I know the drill, so I turn my back to her to allow her some privacy while she quickly undresses. Once she's dressed, she crawls under the covers. "Yeah, who knows? You might meet that special someone. Plus, I would like to help Jess get some people to her event, so it's not a total bust."

I climb into the bed next to her. "Is that what you want? To find someone special."

She stares up at the ceiling for a few beats before turning her head towards me. "I don't know. I haven't really dated anyone since that asshole freshman year who thought he needed to sleep with the entire first floor of the female dorm. So, I guess it wouldn't hurt to see what's out there. But you might meet someone special."

Silence fills the space as I ponder her last sentence. Someone special. What if I already have?

"I got it." Liana sits up and rests on her elbows. "I bet you'll meet someone who piques your interest and if you don't, I'll make you my famous chicken parm."

"You drive a hard bargain because I do love your chicken parm. Alright. Fine."

Liana squeals with excitement. "This is going to be fun! I'll let Jess know we're in tomorrow." She turns over and clicks off the lamp, shrouding the room in darkness. Lying on my back, I stare up towards the ceiling. Speed dating. What have I got myself into?

chapter three
That's a Big, Fat Nope

Liana

"There are so many people here," I say to Mark as I take in the large room. Three long rows of banquet tables fill the space; each could easily fit about twenty-five people. But by the number of people milling around, there must be close to one-hundred people here. Mark stands next to me, a wrinkle creasing his brow. I don't know if he's surprised at the number of people or nervous about being here.

Jess barrels past us, her blonde hair floating behind her, but I catch her before she can get too far. "Hey, this looks like an amazing turn out."

"Thanks. The turnout is much greater than expected. Can you guys help me grab a few more tables?" She wipes the sweat on her brow with her hand.

"Yeah, of course."

We follow Jess to a back room and help her set up the extra tables and chairs to accommodate everyone. Once everyone has taken their seats, Jess steps up to the podium with a microphone. She gives everyone directions on how this will work. We'll have two minutes with each person at our table. After round one, we can write the name of someone we want to talk more with. If they write our name, too, it's a match, and we can go to a separate area to chat. If there isn't a match, we continue to round two and the same thing until round three. Jess sounds the bell, and we begin.

My eyes flicker to the guy who's sitting across from me. He has a warm smile and kind eyes. But after every question I ask him, he asks the same question back. Boring. Next. The bell sounds and the guys rotate. This new guy looks promising, but then I look up at his baseball cap. Date someone whose favorite team is my team's rival? That's a big, fat nope. Up next is a twenty-five-year-old junior with no declared major. The lack of ambition astounds me. Also, nope.

An hour later, the first round is over, and I want to bang my head against the table. Dud after dud made me wonder if it's just better to stay single. Needless to say, I left my piece of paper blank. I pray the next round goes better. This time when I look up, I'm greeted with familiar green eyes and a smile I love to see.

"So, how's it going? Meet the love of your life yet?" Mark rests his elbows on the table as he leans in.

"I think I know why I've been single for the last two years."

Mark releases a hearty laugh. "I hear ya there. One girl I talked to wanted me to be her date for her sister's wedding."

"I call your wedding girl and raise you a guy who lives with his roommates." I raise an eyebrow.

"A lot of college students live with roommates."

"His roommates are his parents. He refers to his parents as his roommates," I deadpan.

"Oh, shit." Mark laughs. "That's very *Grandma's Boy* of him."

"He probably has a race car bed too." Neither of us can hold back our laughter.

"But let's not forget the girl who propositioned me for a threesome."

"How did you turn that down? You and two girls. Hot." I dramatically fan myself with my hand.

"Sadly, it was with the girl and her boyfriend. They wanted to try new things," Mark says using air quotes.

"There's a time and place for everything…"

"And this is not one of them," we both say in unison.

"This is turning out to be a bust. You wanna get out of here?"

I contemplate his idea, but I would hate to bail on Jess. Then it hits me. "Wait. You want to leave just so you can win the bet. I'm on to you." I narrow my eyes at him.

"You got me." He gives me a tight smile.

"We have one more round. Your perfect girl has got to be out there." I sit up straighter as my gaze dances around the room, looking for her. When I circle back to Mark, his forest green eyes are trained on me.

"What?" I ask him quizzically.

"Nothing." Mark casts his eyes downward while he shakes his head. The bell sounds, announcing the change of seats. Mark stands to move to the next chair. When he looks back at me, I mouth good luck. In return, he gives me a stiff smile.

The rest of round two goes as great as round one. I'm

praying round three offers something promising; otherwise, this day will have been a waste and I know Mark won't let me hear the end of it. When the round starts, the first few guys I chat with are nice, but none of them give me those butterflies in my stomach until the third guy sits down. Immediately, I recognized him from one of my business classes last year. Whenever Cade walked into class, he would always catch my eye. Shaggy, dirty-blond hair tucked under a baseball cap. Lean build, but still muscular. I've never taken the opportunity to talk to him until now. Conversation flows easily, as easy as it could in two minutes anyway, and I think I've finally found a winner.

When the third round ends, I scribble Cade's name on the paper and cross my fingers that he wrote mine. The organizers collect all the slips of paper and I stand off to the side waiting until a volunteer comes over with Cade. I can't help the smile that takes over my face.

"Well, I'm glad to see we've made a connection." Cade beams down at me.

"Me too. Wait here for just a moment. I need to find my friend real quick." Cade nods his head in understanding.

I search the large room for Mark, then I spot him along the far wall. My feet carry me to where he's standing. "So, did you connect with anyone?" I bounce on my toes, hoping it's a yes so I won't feel bad about Cade.

"I did, but apparently she didn't feel the same way."

"I'm sorry, Mark." I rest my hand on his forearm.

He studies the spot where I'm touching him, then looks over to where Cade is standing. "But it looks like you have. Better not keep him waiting."

"Yeah, Cade. We actually had a class together last—"

"I don't need an explanation." He tugs his arm away.

"Okay. Well, I'll call you later. I owe you dinner." Mark doesn't look at me. He just nods his head.

I start to walk towards Cade but stop, I turn back to look at Mark, but he's already halfway to the exit. When I turn back around, a smile lights up Cade's face. I plaster on a fake smile in return, but the look of disappointment on Mark's face sits at the forefront of my mind.

chapter four
Everything is Right in the World Again

Liana

Things were still slightly awkward between Mark and me after the speed dating incident. Whenever we talked, it was always one-or-two-word responses from him. Finally, by Thursday night, I told him to come over and I would pay my chicken parm debt. A knock sounds on my front door, and I whip off my apron to answer it. Mark is standing on the other side, his dark hair styled back, a light scruff covering his jawline. Normally, he's pretty clean-shaven, but I like this look on him. Mark holds up a bottle of wine in one hand and a strawberry cheesecake in the other.

"Sorry I've been kind of an ass this week. I bring gifts to make amends." He juts out his bottom lip just slightly. How can I stay mad at that face?

"Apology accepted." I step aside so he can come in and close the door behind him. I grab the bottle of wine and cheesecake from him while he toes off his boots. "Maybe you should be a jerk more often so I get more gifts like this." I peer over my shoulder and flash Mark a playful smile.

Mark shakes his head as he follows me into my narrow kitchen. "It smells delicious in here." The aroma of roasted garlic, stewed tomatoes, rosemary, and basil waft through the room. He pats his stomach as a low grumble sounds from his belly.

"Just a few more minutes and it will be done. Want to open the wine?"

Mark carries himself around the kitchen as if it were his own, knowing where I keep the wine opener and the glasses. The easy way he moves around my space causes my lips to quirk up to the side.

"What's that smirk for?" Mark hands me a glass as he moves to rest his butt against the counter opposite me. He crosses one foot over the other and sets his glass of wine on the laminate countertop.

"It's… nothing." I bow my head as I butter the bread for garlic toast.

"Were you thinking of Cade?" This is the first time since last weekend that Mark has mentioned him. I figured he would just be a topic of conversation we would avoid. It's not like we are anything serious. We're just getting to know each other.

"Actually, no." I grab the pan of garlic bread and set it in the oven. Turning around, I mimic Mark's pose. "I was thinking how seamlessly you fit in my space. It's like you belong here."

"Lee, are you getting all sentimental on me?" Mark

pushes off the counter and within two steps, he's standing in front of me.

I crane my neck to look at him. "No." I take a deep breath to collect my thoughts. "I'm just saying I don't know what I would do if you weren't in my life. You're my best friend."

The look on Mark's face falls, and he takes a step back. "Right. Your best friend."

Before I can ask him what he means by that comment, the ding from the timer for the food interrupts us. Next to the kitchen is a small dining room with a modest four-person table. Mark works on setting the table while I get the food onto serving trays. We sit down for dinner and make small talk. Whatever happened previously in the kitchen is forgotten, but a lingering awkwardness still hanging above us.

After dinner, we sit in the living room and turn on a movie. I'm curled up on one side of the couch while Mark sits on the other end. My phone buzzes in my lap and I flip open my phone to check the message. When I look up, Mark is staring at me. "Cade?"

"No, actually my brother wants to know if we want to go to The Sports Den tomorrow with him and Trey to watch the game?"

Relief washes over Mark's face. "Yeah. Sounds great."

"Perfect, I'll let him know." My fingers type out a message back to my brother. "Are you ready for cheesecake?" Before he can answer, I rise to my feet and walk into the kitchen. I grab the cheesecake from the fridge and open the drawer to collect two forks. When I enter the living room, Mark sits up on the couch. I sit on the cushion next to him and place the cheesecake on my lap while I hold out a fork to him. Mark scoots closer, his thigh touching mine. The contact makes me pause and look in his direction.

"So, you just bring the whole thing in here?" Mark asks.

"Yep."

"I like your style."

We both dig in. My lips close around the fork and I can't help the moan that escapes. When I glance over, Mark is staring at me with his heaping pile of cheesecake in front of his face.

"What? This is the best cheesecake," I mumble around my mouth full of the soft and creamy sweet treat. I swallow down the last bite and lick my lips. "You need to try it with one of these strawberries." I dig into the cheesecake again, taking a slice of strawberry with it. I hold it up towards Mark. He leans forward and takes the bite off my fork. "I missed this. Missed us."

"What are you talking about?"

"Earlier in the week. We barely talked to each other, and we've never not talked to each other for that long. I didn't like it."

"Well, no worries." He dips his pointer finger into one of the whipped cream dollops circling the edge of the cheesecake and smears it on my cheek. A big boyish grin covers his face. "Everything is right in the world again."

"Hey!" I dip my finger in the whipped cream and dab it on his nose. He stares me down, and for a brief moment, the corner of his eyes crinkle. Before I know what's happening, he smears a handful of cheesecake down my cheek as I let out a squeal of laughter. Within seconds, cheesecake is being flung back and forth. The strawberry syrup is dripping down my cleavage and crumbles of graham cracker litter my hair. There's cheesecake on the couch, on the floor, on the walls, even some on the ceiling.

Once the tray is empty, Mark and I lie on the floor in a fit of laughter. I turn towards Mark, cheesecake covering his face. I swipe my finger down his cheek, scooping up some of the soft filling and sucking it off my finger. He fixates on my finger as I pull it out of my mouth. "Still tastes good."

chapter five
Not-So-Best Friendly Thoughts

Mark

"This is from the guy sitting over there." The bartender sets a pint of beer in front of Liana and nods to the left. She swivels around to check out the guy and offers a silent thank you before turning around.

"He's in my art history class. I never noticed before but he's kinda cute." Liana takes a sip of her beer.

We're sitting at the bar of The Sports Den, the pre-game broadcasted on the row of TVs above us. I'm on the left with Liana next to me. Her brother, Bennett, and his buddy Trey on the end. I met Bennett and Trey my sophomore year when they came to Harbor Highlands College as freshmen. Liana and Bennett have always been close, just eighteen months apart, so it wasn't surprising that they ended up at the same college together.

Trey leans forward, eyes trained on Liana. "Do guys always buy you drinks?"

I slap the bar top, turning to Trey. "Dude, I said the same thing."

"Well, shit. I have to buy my own drinks and pretend they're from girls." Trey sits back and crosses his arms over his chest, pretending to pout.

With a grin covering her face, Liana shakes her head at Trey, then shrugs. "I wouldn't say always. They try to butter me up before coming over to talk. For me, it often leads nowhere, but I'm not going to turn down a free drink." Liana grins into her beer as she takes another sip. "You know what? I'll be back. I have to use the restroom." Liana pushes her stool back. She rests her hand on my shoulder to help her balance as she walks behind me. I glance to where she just touched me, and then instinctively, I look up to my left as she saunters to the other side of the room where the restrooms are located. I'm mesmerized by the hypnotic way her ass sways with each step in her tight as fuck jeans. The sound of someone calling my name pulls me out of my Liana trance.

"Dude, if you stare any harder, I think your eyes might pop out," Trey says.

"I don't know what you're talking about." I reach for my beer and take a big gulp, needing something to calm my erratic heartbeat.

"We've been calling your name for the past thirty seconds and crickets." Bennett raises an eyebrow at me.

Trey leans over, resting his elbows on the bar to look at me. "You got the hots for Liana. You want her to stroke your bat and fondle your balls."

"No one is playing with my balls," I say a little too loudly based on the strange looks from the patrons sitting behind Trey. Heat creeps up my neck before I give him a slight headshake needing to get my mind off her fondling my balls. "She's my best friend. I was just making sure no creeps were stalking her."

"I'm pretty sure you just had some not-so-best friendly thoughts pass through your head. If you know what I mean." Trey wiggles his eyebrows.

Bennett punches him in the arm. "Hey, that's my sister you're talking about."

"I'm just saying Mark would be a better candidate than some of the other guys out there." Trey rubs his hand over his bicep.

"Yeah, sure. But I don't need to know what they do behind closed doors," Bennett says.

"Hey, I'm right here." I look them both in the eyes. "Look, nothing's happening between us. No closed doors. Nothing." But he's not wrong. On many occasions it's *her* face that manifests in my late-night fantasies. But it's never good to mix friends with pleasure.

Bennett leans over and looks me square in the eyes. "But know she's my sister. If anything happens and you hurt her, I'll kick your ass." He leans back. "But like Trey said, you're better suited for her than anyone I can think of, so you have my blessing."

Just then Liana comes back, pulls out her stool and hops up. "What did I miss? Did they announce the starting line-up yet?" Her gaze darts between all three of us, her brow crinkle in confusion. Trey takes a big gulp of his beer as Bennett picks at an imaginary spot on the wood bar top. "Okay. What's going on? You guys are acting weird," Liana says as she turns to me.

"Nothing," I reply. "You haven't missed any announcements." Seeming satisfied with my answer, Liana turns her attention to Bennett and I exhale a sigh of relief, glad she didn't pry anymore because I wouldn't be able to keep up with the lie.

"So baby bro, you dating anyone? Because it would be fantastic if game nights featured more estrogen and less testosterone." Liana nudges Bennett's ribs.

Bennett rolls his eyes before taking a swig of his beer. "Sorry to disappoint but having a girlfriend is nowhere on my radar."

"Maybe just a little blip on your radar?" Liana holds up her thumb and pointer finger centimeters apart from each other.

"I have bigger plans than settling down with a girlfriend. I can't afford that kind of distraction"

Trey turns toward Bennett and says, "Like the blonde distraction that left your room this morning."

Liana's gaze shoots to Bennett and tilts her head waiting for an explanation.

He releases a hearty laugh before shrugging his shoulders. "I said no girlfriends. Nothing about not doing other things."

Trey clasps him on the shoulder, and Liana directs her attention back to me. Her chocolate brown eyes lock onto mine.

"At least I have you here to keep me sane."

I give her a small smile because I don't know what I would do without her in my life. Now, I have Bennett's and Trey's comments swimming through my mind, but everything comes back to her being my best friend. I can't lose that. Luckily, the game starts, and we glue our eyes to the television. All talk about best friends, Liana, balls, and closed doors are extinguished.

Several innings in, Trey leans over, eyes trained on Liana.

"Liana, so all these guys buy you drinks at the bar. You

two do this bet thing all the time." Trey shifts his finger between Liana and me. "I bet you won't kiss the next guy who buys you a drink. I got twenty dollars on it." Trey pulls out his wallet and slaps a twenty-dollar bill on the bar top. I narrow my eyes at him. What the hell is Trey doing?

Liana releases a laugh. "The bets are our thing." She points between her and me. "What makes you think you can just hop on the bet train?"

"Because I know you can't turn down a bet or twenty dollars." Trey pushes the bill closer to Liana. When she reaches for it, Trey tugs it back. "Gotta win the bet first. But also, if I win, you owe me."

Liana sighs, pretending like this is such a chore for her. "Deal, but only because I've been eyeing this really cute pair of Uggs."

A moment later, Trey calls the bartender over and he leans across the bar to whisper in her ear. The bartender turns to look at Liana, then back to Trey before nodding. Trey sits back down, a Cheshire grin covering his face.

Several more innings pass along with several more drinks. I swallow down the last of my beer, set the glass on the top and push it toward the other edge of the bar. Trey and Bennett finish theirs as well.

"Seventh inning. Time for another round. Mark's buying," Trey announces to the bartender. She collects four glasses and lines them up across the rail. One by one, she pulls down the tap to fill the pint glasses.

"Okay. Okay. But someone else is getting the next round." I fish out my wallet to grab some cash. The bartender carries all four beers, sets them down in front of us, and then disperses them. I hand over the cash and tell her to keep the change. Everyone reaches for their beer and takes a drink.

Before I can even swallow, Trey throws his chair back

and points at me. "You, my friend, are our lucky suitor." Bennett turns toward us and busts out laughing. Liana looks at them, then at me with a confused look on her face.

I finally swallow my beer and set the glass down. "Dude, what are you talking about?"

"The bet. She has to kiss the next guy who buys her a drink." A wide grin spreads across Trey's face.

"No. No. No. That doesn't count," Liana interjects, shaking her head back and forth.

"Come on, man. She doesn't have to do it," I say. Turning to Liana, I tell her, "We don't have to do this."

"No. You're right. She doesn't. But a bet's a bet, so I'll take my twenty bucks if she's not doing it." Trey holds out his hand and wiggles his fingers with the cockiest grin on his face.

Liana stares at her beer in front of her, contemplating what she should do. It's like she's waiting for one of the carbonation bubbles to float up and give her all the answers. Finally, she turns toward me. "But I want my boots. Do it for the boots?" Her brown doe eyes stare into mine. "It's just a kiss. We can do this."

I'm not sure if she's giving me a pep talk or herself. I rub the palms of my hands on my jeans. I can do this. She's just my best friend. A best friend I've fantasized about doing this with many times. Liana turns her body towards mine so her legs are between my spread ones. I peer past Liana and see Bennett and Trey staring intently at us, wondering if this is actually going to happen. Liana lifts her hands at the same time I lift mine. We fumble back and forth. I'm sure to everyone else it looks like slow-motion karate chops. It's as if we're teenagers going in for our first kiss. But essentially, this is our first kiss. Finally, Liana stops our hand dance when she grabs mine and rests them on my thighs.

"There. Much better. Now, I don't feel like you're going to smack me in the face." My eyes meet hers before her hands reach up to gently cup my cheeks. One side of her lip tips up, probably because of the scruff tickling her delicate skin as she lightly caresses my stubble. Just then, her tongue peeks out and wets her lips. At that moment, I forget to breathe. The world around me goes silent, except for my heart pounding in my ears. She leans in, her lips a mere centimeter away from mine. I go all in, leaning forward the rest of the way until our lips touch.

chapter six
I Just Kissed My Best Friend

Liana

My entire body feels weightless. The only thing keeping me grounded is the point of contact between Mark's lips and mine. There's a shift in the atmosphere as soon as our lips connect. Like a cloud of lightning needing to expel all that energy. Everything around me is quiet. All I can concentrate on is this kiss. At first, his lips are soft but he must feel it too because he deepens the kiss, and I let him. This is a feeling I've never felt before and it's all caused by my best friend. When I feel him pull away, I drop my hands. My eyelids slowly flutter open. A sliver of green outlines his dilated pupils. Instinctively, my fingertips come up to rest on the spot his lips once were. Mark's lips upturn on one side as he watches me. I just kissed my best friend. Suddenly an eruption of cheers and people hooting and hollering breaks us from our kiss-induced trance. Our attention shoots to the TV screen to see our team got a home run.

Bennett nudges me with his elbow, giving me a cheesy grin. When I look over to Trey, he's sliding the twenty across the bar top. Our eyes connect, and he gives me a wink. I can't stop the smile on my face as heat creeps up my cheeks. I snag the bill and shove it in my pocket. As I look back up, I peek a glance at Mark. Straight nose. Strong jaw line. Full, pouty lips that I want on mine again.

The rest of the night carries on like any other bar and baseball night, except this time I can't stop thinking about Mark's lips on mine. I've had many first kisses before, but this one was different. Electrifying. It made me feel alive. And I want to do it all over again.

The next day, I'm waiting for Mark's class to end outside the lecture hall, perched on the window ledge as the warm sun heats my skin. While skimming notes for my class later this afternoon, a girl calls my name, drawing my attention from my notebook. When I look up, Marisa is standing in front of me. I've seen her at a few parties. She frequents the rugby house, so she must be friends with some of the guys, or at least friendly with the guys.

"Hey, Marisa. How are you?" I close my notebook and set it to the side.

"Good. But I'm ready for this semester to be over already." Marisa holds the straps of her backpack as she shifts her weight from foot to foot. She's a cute girl with shoulder-length blonde hair with a natural beach wave. Bright blue eyes and a killer smile that I'm sure gets all the guys to fawn all over her. She's more petite than me. Maybe around five-one compared to my five-five.

"I get that. I have to get through this last year, then I graduate, but I'm definitely ready for it to be over."

Marisa nods her head. Uncertainty stirs behind her eyes like she wants to ask me something, but doesn't know how. Her teeth sink into her bottom lip before asking, "I have a question for you?"

I raise an eyebrow at her, my gut knowing where this is going before she even says anything because she isn't the first one. It's always let's ask the best friend to hook us up. *She's a girl. She'll get it.* Mark's an attractive guy, so it's no wonder he would have girls interested in him. But what they don't know is they'll get more mileage out of their ask if they approach him directly versus using his best friend. "What can I help you with, Marisa?" I try to keep the sarcasm out of my voice but fail.

"Well, I know you're friends with Mark. I was just wondering if you could give him my number?"

Plastering on a fake smile, I say, "Yeah. Sure. I can give it to him." *Or I can throw it in the trash.*

Excitement lights up her eyes and I want to roll mine. "That would be amazing. Can I use your pen and a piece of paper?" Her eyes cut to my notebook next to me. I rip off a piece of paper and hand it to her with a pen. She scribbles her name and number down before passing it back. "Thank you so much. You're the best Liana." She turns on her heel and saunters away.

I open the folded piece of paper and trace the loops in her handwriting and the heart drawn at the end. I crumble it up and shove it in my pocket, contemplating if I should just throw it in the trash. But I think better of it. She's a nice girl. Mark might actually like her, and that thought puts a sour taste in my mouth.

Thirty minutes later, Mark's figure appears in the doorway. As soon as he sees me, a small smile graces his lips and he gives me a head nod. He finishes a conversation with a classmate before weaving in and out of students to meet me across the hallway. I pack up my bag and stand. We join the crowd of students as we walk in comfortable silence through the halls of the different buildings to get to the food court. Being in Northern Minnesota, the best thing about this campus is that all the buildings are connected by hallways, skywalks, and an underground tunnel that connects the on-campus dorms. There is no need to go outside, which is a major selling point come winter.

As we enter the food court, the piece of paper with Marisa's number scribbled on it and her dumb hand-drawn heart burns a hole in my pocket. Fishing it out, I hold my open palm out to Mark, the ball of paper nestled in the center.

"Here. I'm supposed to give this to you."

Mark's eyebrows knit together as he looks down. "What's that?"

"A phone number. Take it." I try to keep my tone neutral but fail miserably at keeping the bitterness at bay. Why am I so upset over a phone number? I shouldn't be. *Maybe because you two shared a mind-blowing kiss the other night and now you don't know how to process these feelings you have for your best friend?* Shut up, conscience. Stop making sense.

Mark unfolds the paper. "Oh look, a heart." He holds out the wrinkled paper to me while pointing at the drawing.

"Yeah. Isn't that precious? I think I'm going to grab a soup and sandwich." Walking toward the sandwich stand, I get in line with several other students. I say a silent prayer that Mark picks something else so I can have a few moments with my thoughts, but instead he trails right behind me.

"When did she give you this?" Mark stands next to me, still holding the phone number.

"While I was waiting for you to finish class. I think I'm going to have the turkey club. Maybe I'll make it a wrap." I look up at the menu board with my finger tapping on my chin.

"I didn't know she was interested in me. Do you think I should call her?"

With a huff, I turn to Mark. "Look. I don't know. If you like her, call her." My words come out more harshly than I intended.

"What's up with you today?" Mark tucks the piece of paper into his pocket. His gaze is firmly planted on me while I watch him from the corner of my eye.

"Nothing. I just need something to eat." I turn my head slightly to catch a glimpse of Mark, a smile tugging on his lips.

He looks up at the menu board. "You do get pretty hangry when you haven't eaten."

I backhand him in the stomach, and I hear his oomph as he clutches the spot I just smacked. "Shush." When we reach the counter, we order our food and find an empty table along the back wall.

Students mill around and chatter while enjoying their à la carte meals. I unwrap my sandwich and take a bite while Mark, sitting across from me, does the same. We eat in silence, unsure of what to say. I think this is the first time both of us have been at a loss for words.

"Hey Liana. I'm glad I found you here."

I look up and I'm greeted by a dazzling smile from a familiar face. "Hey, Cade. How's it going?" From my periphery, I watch as Mark flits his gaze between Cade and me. I'm sure he's wondering what he's doing here because I'm wondering the same thing. We've talked once or twice since the speed dating night, but nothing really took flight.

"It's going good. I wanted to invite you to a party tonight at my house."

"Oh, a party. Yeah. That sounds fun." I give him an over-the-top fake smile.

"Great." He rattles off his address and gives me a time. Before he leaves, he turns to Mark. "Hey man, you can come too. More the merrier."

Mark gives him a head nod. "Great. Thanks. Sounds like a good time."

"It's always a good time at Casa de Cade." He winks at me before turning around to meet back up with his buddies on the other side of the food court.

"Casa de Cade? What the fuck is that?" Mark chuckles before taking another bite of his sandwich. "Are you actually going?" he asks after he swallows.

"Sure, why not? It's Friday night. Plus, it would be kinda rude to turn down the invite now." I shrug one shoulder. But if you ask me to stay in so we binge-watch whatever season we're on of *The Office*, I will totally do that instead.

Mark stares down at his plate of food before lifting his eyes to mine. Green irises with flecks of gold bore into me as he contemplates his words. "Alright. Maybe I'll give Marisa a call. See if she's interested in a party tonight." He continues to stare me down, waiting for any type of reaction.

"Yeah. You should do that," I say, not taking the bait. "I'll be with Cade, and you'll be with Marisa. It will be a great time." Suddenly, not feeling hungry anymore, I collect my bag, throw one strap over my shoulder and stand. "I totally forgot I have some research I need to finish up for a paper. I'm going to go to the library and do that before my next class. But call me later and we'll head over to the party." Before Mark can reply, I grab my tray as my feet swiftly carry me toward the exit. I dump my half-eaten sandwich and untouched soup into the trash and toss my tray on top. Then I'm out the door without a single glance back.

chapter seven
It's Always Been You

Mark

Why did I say I would invite Marisa? Another party I really don't want to go to, but also, I don't want Liana going by herself, especially with Cade. When I asked around about him, I was told he likes to sleep around. New party. Different girl. Apparently, this week he has his sight set on Liana. *Not on my watch.* Liana has a good head on her shoulders, but something about that guy doesn't sit well with me.

Let's not forget her odd behavior at lunch today. It makes me wonder if she's having the same thoughts as I am. Because ever since the kiss at the bar, I haven't been able to get her out of my mind. These aren't platonic thoughts, either. My eyes drift closed as I imagine her soft lips on mine while I wrap my arms around her body and press her to me. The way she would moan as I drag my tongue down the column of her neck and press open mouth kisses across her chest. I fantasize about what her breasts would feel like as I cup them in my hands while I brush my fingertip across her hardening nipples. Fuck. I pop open my eyelids and turn toward the clock on the wall, wondering if I have time to rub one out before she arrives. Just then my phone buzzes, and I flip it open to read a text.

Liana: Almost to your place.

My gaze drifts up to the ceiling while my hand adjusts my thickening dick in my pants. Just what I need is for Liana to meet me with a boner. I rattle off baseball stats to myself to calm down. After a few minutes, I stand from the couch and pull open the front door. The warm fall evening air greets me first. To my surprise, Liana is already waiting for me on my porch. Her silky, soft hair twirls around her shoulder, and her bright chocolate brown eyes meet mine as she turns to me.

"Hey." A smile lights up her face.

God, I love that smile.

"Hey yourself."

She tilts her head at me. "You okay? You look a little flushed."

"Uh, yeah. I'm great. Let's go." I push the rest of the way out the door and close it behind me, sending up a silent prayer that either my bulge has dissipated or she doesn't notice.

My house is the halfway point between Liana's and Cade's, so the walk isn't too bad. People are already staggering down the middle of the road and on the sidewalk, and we're still a block away. The music gets louder and louder the closer we get.

"So is Marisa meeting you here?" Liana asks, breaking the silence.

"Yeah. I invited her. Told her where it was. We'll see if she shows up." Liana's face remains stoic as she continues to look forward. I'm desperate to know what she's thinking right now.

"I wanted to talk to you about something."

"Yeah?" She turns, her eyebrows raise.

"I asked around about Cade. A couple of guys mentioned he sleeps around and—"

Liana leans away from me, crossing her arms over her chest. "Thanks for your concern, but I'm a big girl. I can take care of myself."

Exhaling a breath, I tip my head up to the inky sky. "I know. I just wanted you to know."

The rest of the walk is silent until we finally reach Cade's house. I gesture for Liana to go in ahead of me. As soon as we walk in the front door, the pungent smell of stale beer and pot smoke smacks us in our faces. People fill every nook and cranny available. A group huddles around, cheering while someone does a beer bong, and another small group passes a joint. We squeeze our way in and out of crowds of people until we find a small unoccupied area.

"Wait here. I'll go find us some beers," I say as "Crazy Bitch" by Buckcherry blasts from the speakers. Liana just nods at me. After locating the keg, I fill up two cups, and bring them over to Liana. Luckily, she's still standing where I left her. Partygoers mill around the room. Some are dancing on the floor, while others have taken to the furniture. Like a bloodhound, Cade doesn't take long to sniff out Liana.

"Hey, there she is. The most beautiful girl here," Cade slurs as he throws his arm around Liana's shoulder.

She beams up at him. "Hey. Great turn out tonight."

"Yeah. Glad you guys could make it." He holds his cup out to me to cheers. I bump mine with his. Then he looks down at Liana. "I got a couple of people for you to meet."

Liana nods her head before turning to me. "Will you be okay by yourself for a bit?"

"Yeah. Go ahead. I'll just wait for Marisa." I take a sip of my beer.

While they walk away, Cade's arm wraps around Liana, and he looks back over his shoulder and winks at me. What the fuck was that for? Something about that guy doesn't sit right with me.

Several beers later, Liana still hasn't made her way back yet, but someone else found me. Marisa drones on and on about who knows what while I constantly scan the room, looking for Liana. A conversation to my left catches my attention. Something about Cade, a girl, and a bedroom. Interrupting whatever Marisa is yammering on about, I take a few strides to where the two guys are talking.

"What did you just say? About Cade?" I glare at them.

"Dude just took a hot brunette into his room. The chick was wasted," one guy says.

"That guy gets all the hot ones." The other guy cheers his beer with the first guy.

All I see is red. They say to always trust your gut, and right from the start, I knew Cade was trouble. Liana was never one for random hookups with guys. That's not her style, and she wouldn't start now. I toss my cup to the ground, beer splattering everywhere. All I hear is 'what the fuck, man' from behind me as my legs propel me through the crowd to find the stairs. I take them two at a time, and once I reach the top, I pause a moment to catch my breath. I stare down a dimly lit hallway lined with closed doors. The only bright light comes from the one open door that leads to a bathroom. Fuck. Which door is his? Well, time to find out. I throw open doors, beginning with the one closest to me. Each one is as empty as the last. When I get to the last door, my hand rests on the doorknob. I can hear the murmur of voices from the other side. Twisting the knob, I shove open the door, and my heart stops. In the dark, all I see is the silhouette of a guy on top of a girl in the middle of a bed. Then I hear her voice. I would know that voice anywhere.

"Stop. Get off me." There's anguish in her tone as she tries to push him off.

"Oh. Come on. You'll like it." He knocks her hands away to bend down to get closer to her.

In a few quick strides, my feet pound against the wood floor until I'm standing at the foot of the bed. My hand digs into the collar of the guy's shirt, ripping him backward. His body flies off the bed, his back hitting a dresser, and then he scrambles to his feet.

"What the fuck!" Cade roars, but I ignore him. My only concern is Liana.

She screams while scrambling to the head of the bed. "Liana. Are you alright?"

Before she can respond, Cade grabs my shoulder and wrenches me around. "What the hell are you doing, man? We are just having a good time."

"Yeah. Didn't sound like she was having a good time." I turn my attention back to Liana, but Cade grabs me again, fingers digging into my bicep, as he twists me around. Just as I swing around, a fist connects with my jaw. Fuck. That hurt. I stumble backward before collecting my bearings. A metallic tang fills my mouth.

Cade comes after me again, but I lower my shoulder and charge until his back slams into a wall with an oomph. With him stunned, I pull my arm back and swing, my fist connecting with this face. I take another shot to his gut. His body crumbles to the ground as he groans.

I run back to the side of the bed to Liana. Pain shoots to my fingertips as I clench and unclench my hand, but I can't worry about that now. She needs me more. Tears stream down her cheeks. "Hey, you alright?" She just nods at me. I scan her body, making a quick assessment that she really is okay. "Let's get out of here." I lift her to her feet and wrap my arms around her.

A crowd has formed in the hallway outside the bedroom, and I push people out of the way so we can get out of here. When we get outside, the cool air hits my face. My busted lip throbs.

"Mark. I'm so sorry." Her body racks with a sob.

"Hey, shh. It's okay. No need to be sorry. You didn't do anything wrong." My hand brushes up and down her arm as she cries into my chest.

The rest of the walk is silent until we reach the sidewalk that leads up to my house. I look down at Liana. Most of her tears have dried, but I reach up with my thumb and wipe away the last bit of wetness. "Do you want me to walk you the rest of the way to your house or do you wanna crash in my bed?"

Her brown eyes search mine for a moment. "Honestly, if you don't mind, I would rather not be alone right now."

I nod and steer her the rest of the way up to my house. When we're inside, and in my room, I dig around in my dresser for a t-shirt and a pair of sweatpants for her. I set them on the bed and close the door behind me to give her some privacy to change. A few minutes later, I crack open the door and peek my head through. Her clothes lay in a pile on the floor next to the bed. Liana is under the covers. The soft glow from the lamp lighting up her face.

"I'm just going to sleep on the couch. Do you need anything else?"

"You're not going to sleep in here?" Her teeth sink into her bottom lip.

Fuck. My fingers comb through my hair, tugging at the strands. Why can't I say no to this girl? "Do you want me to sleep in here?"

She just nods her head. I squeeze through the crack and close the door behind me. The soft click is the only sound that fills the room. My feet carry me to the opposite side of the bed. I pull back the covers and crawl inside, lying on my back. Liana reaches over to the lamp and switches it off, encasing the room in darkness. A streetlamp outside shines through the cracks in the blinds, offering just enough light to not be pitch black. I hear a soft sniffle to my left and I turn on my side to face her.

"Liana. You alright?" My voice is soft.

"Yeah." She sniffles again and turns to face me. "I just keep thinking about what happened. What could have happened if you weren't there." Her hand goes up to swipe across her cheek.

"Come here." I reach for her and pull her to me. She buries her head into my chest as freshly fallen tears stain my shirt. But I don't care. All I care about is that she's safe. "I got you. I'll never leave you." My hand rubs small circles across her back. After several minutes, when her sniffles subside and I think she's fallen asleep, she speaks.

"Mark?" Her voice a quiet whisper.

"Yeah?"

"Thank you."

The back of her fingers trails along my cotton-covered stomach until they're splayed over my waist. The bed dips slightly as she pushes herself upward. Suddenly, warm, soft lips are on mine. My body freezes instantly. She's kissing me. Her fingers move to my back, tugging herself closer, her warm body presses up against mine. Her once soft kisses become more demanding. She needs to expel the events from tonight out of her head. I don't blame her. I kiss her back because I've wanted this for so long. Her soft moan fills the quiet room. All I've wanted to do since the night at the bar is kiss this girl again. But I can't. Not like this.

I pull away. "Wait. I can't do this." Her face falls as she pushes away from me to sit up. "No. No. I want to do this. God, I've wanted to do this for so long. You have no idea." I rake my hands through my hair before turning to her. "But I don't want to do it like this. We've been drinking. You just went through all that bullshit with Cade."

"It's because of that bullshit that I realize it's you I want to be with. It's always been you. I don't want to be with anyone else. I've denied these feelings for you for so long, but I'm done fighting them." There's a pleading tone in her voice.

I grab her and pull her to me, and she comes willingly. My arms wrap around her. "God, you don't know how bad I needed to hear you say that." I press a kiss on her forehead. "But how about this? Let's go to sleep and see if you feel the same way come morning." I feel her head nod against my chest. They often say a person is more honest when they've been drinking, and I hope that is true because she just told me everything I've been waiting for. Eventually, we both fall asleep with her still wrapped in my arms.

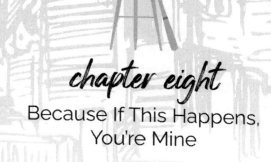

chapter eight
Because If This Happens, You're Mine

Liana

The morning light shines through the blinds, causing me to stir awake. I'm snuggled next to a warm body, then it hits me. The events from last night flash through my mind. But the big one I focus on is I want to be with Mark, and he wants to be with me. Butterflies erupt and take flight in my belly at the thought. Slowly, I pull away, careful not to wake him, making my way to the bathroom. I do my business and freshen up with a capful of mouthwash, knowing it's his because he's the only person I know who uses pink mouthwash. When I return, Mark is awake, sitting up, back resting against the wall. His hair is a messy brown mop on top of his head. I just want to run my fingers through it. Closing the door behind me, I saunter towards the bed before climbing on, sitting on my knees.

"Good morning."

"Morning," I pause. "So about last night…" He swallows and I watch his Adam's apple bob up and down before I continue. "I still feel the same way."

A smile tugs at his lips. "Yeah?"

All I can do is nod before I lift a leg to crawl onto his lap. My hands cup his face as I bring my lips down to his. This is all I've ever wanted. He is all I've ever needed. And finally, he's mine. The kiss starts off innocent but quickly turns heated. His tongue peeks out to part my lips, and I let him. My fingers comb through his shaggy locks while his hands roam across my back under his shirt I'm wearing, his fingertips leaving a heated trail in their wake. I grip a handful of his hair and tug, forcing his mouth closer to mine. A deep growl rumbles through his chest, which spurs me on more. I rub my chest against his. The cotton fabric from my shirt brushes against my hardened nipples sending a jolt of pleasure to my core.

"Wait," Mark mumbles with his lips still on mine. *Oh God, not this again.* I pull away to look him in the eyes. Desire and lust pool in his irises. "I need to get this blanket off me."

I scramble to get off him so he can remove the blanket. This time, he tugs me down on the bed, his body hovering over mine. I spread my legs, giving him room to nestle between them. His green eyes search mine before asking, "Are you sure? Because if this happens, you're mine. I'm never letting you go."

I have no words to express how I feel, so I just reach up and wrap my arms around his neck and tug him down to me. Putting all my thoughts and feelings into this one kiss. Because I never want to let him go, and I never want him to let me go. His lips move from mine to kiss my cheek and then down to my neck, his light stubble tickles my sensitive skin as he goes. He lifts himself up, his hands reach for the hem of my shirt, and he tugs upwards. With my naked breasts exposed to him, he stares as if he's seen nothing more beautiful in the world. My heartbeats erratically in my chest. I've never felt so vulnerable in my entire life. His gentle hand cups one breast while he rolls my nipple between his fingers. His mouth descends on the other breast, pressing kisses to my soft flesh. I can't help the moan that escapes while I arch my back, wanting more. Needing more.

Mark sits back and tugs his shirt off with one hand. I finish removing mine at the same time. Unable to help myself, I take a moment to admire his bare chest, defined pecs, and tapered waist. Sure, I've seen him shirtless before but never like this, hovering over me, hunger in his eyes like he wants to devour me. I wrap my hand around his waist and tug him back to me, wanting to feel his bare skin on mine. This time, the bulge in his shorts is more prominent as he grinds against my aching pussy. I want to feel him. All of him. My fingers find the elastic waistband and slip underneath. I drag my hands over the firm muscle of his ass, taking his shorts with me. He gets the hint and uses a free hand to help me remove them the rest of the way. I use this time to tug down my sweatpants. Once they're over my hips, Mark takes over, drags them down my legs, and tosses them to the floor. I take a moment to take in his fully naked body. Best friends aren't supposed to kiss and definitely aren't supposed to admire each other's naked bodies. But I think it's safe to say we are no longer just best friends.

In an instant, his lips crash against mine, and I relish the feel of his body covering mine. His hand skates down my ribs, over my hips, until his fingers find my neatly trimmed pussy. His fingers spread me wide as he smears my wetness around.

"Fuck. I want you so bad." Mark's hot breath whispers against my neck as his hard cock digs into my hip. One finger pushes inside of me and I release a needy moan. His finger pumps in and out of me a few times before he adds a second finger to the mix and then a third. My hips buck with each thrust of his hand, and I know I'm close. Mark shifts his hand so his thumb can rub my clit while his fingers move inside me. That slight change sets me off. My eyes clamp shut as I ride out the orgasm that washes over my body. When I slowly lift my eyelids, Mark's forest green eyes stare back at me.

"That is a sight I will never grow tired of." He bends down and presses a soft kiss to my lips.

When he pulls away, I bite my lower lip before asking, "Do you have a condom?" His eyes search mine, unsure at first of what I'm really asking.

"In the nightstand."

He rolls to his side as I twist to pull open the drawer. Retrieving a foil packet, I tear it open with my teeth and around, hiking a leg over Mark to straddle his thighs. His hooded eyes watch in fascination as I take out the condom and roll it down his hard cock. When my fingers reach the base and give it a squeeze, he groans. With the condom in place, I sit up and guide his cock to my opening. I slowly slide down, savoring the stretch of his thickness inside me. When I'm fully seated, I look up to Mark. His eyes are pinched closed, his lips are parted, taking in the feeling just like I am.

"Fuck. Lee. You feel so fucking amazing." His hand moves to my hips, and his fingertips leave dimples in my flesh to halt my movements. I begin to move, but he stops me. "Just let me feel you like this for just a second longer."

When his moment is over, his hands guide me to move, so I do. At first, my movement is slow and rhythmic but quickly turns frantic as my second orgasm builds in my core. Mark's hands knead my breast as I ride his cock. Moans escape me every time he thrusts his hips upward. Just as I'm about to detonate, Mark sits up and flips us over, so now he's on top. His hips piston as he sinks in and out, causing a tingling sensation to build in my spine again. Within moments, my release takes over my body as I moan Mark's name. His own orgasm follows a few seconds after mine. His movements slow until he stills inside of me. Emerald green eyes meet mine and in that moment, I've never felt so loved in my entire life. His lips meet mine for a gentle kiss.

"I love you, Liana Marie Pierce."

"I love you, Mark Logan West."

epilogue
Two Years Later

Mark

We walk down the stairs of the crowded baseball stadium to find our seats. Each of us has a beer in one hand and a hot dog in the other. Once we find our row, we sidestep past the other fans until we get to our seats.

"I can't believe it took us this long to finally attend a game in person." Liana sets her drink in the cupholder. I watch as she takes the phallic-shaped food item and puts it in her mouth. A moan escapes her lips, one I'm all too familiar with, and my dick twitches. "What?" she asks around a mouth full of food.

I shake my head and laugh. "Nothing."

"I can't help it. It tastes so good. Why don't these taste this good when we make them at home?"

Home. We both sublet our rooms once the semester

was over, and I asked Liana to move in with me. We found a reasonable one-bedroom apartment close to campus but more in a residential neighborhood versus the college student one. While we still attended the occasional party now and then, we much preferred to stay in. Not going out also helped avoid any run-ins with Cade. The last we heard he was charged with fifth-degree criminal sexual conduct. That time there were witnesses and a security video. But now that we've both graduated and found jobs in the area, I think it's time to take the next step. Instinctively, my hand skims over my pocket to feel the outline of a black velvet box. Liana is the girl I want to spend the rest of my life with. A part of me knew the moment I saw her, but I spent too many years denying those feelings. While I wish our feelings didn't come to the surface the way they did, I still wouldn't change the outcome.

We spend the next hour watching the game while I build up the courage to ask this girl to marry me. I turn to look at my girl. Her brown hair tucked under a baseball cap, the sun shining behind her, creating an almost halo effect. She's definitely my angel.

She turns to me, catching me staring. "What? Do I have something on my face?" Her fingers brush around her lips.

"I love you."

She pauses her actions. "I love you, too." She leans over, and I meet her halfway for a kiss. When she turns back toward the field, she points to the jumbotron. My gaze follows to where she's pointing. A big *Will You Marry Me?* flashes on the screen. Liana sits up in her seat to find the couple with the over-the-top proposal. When her eyes meet my wide-eyed ones, her jaw drops. Apparently, someone else had the same idea as me today.

"I guess another happy couple is trying to steal my

thunder, so no better time than now," I mutter under my breath. Liana stares at me, her eyebrows squished together. I clasp her hands with mine. "You're my best friend, and I swear I love you more and more with each passing day. I wouldn't be the man I am today without you. So, I have a question for you." Releasing her, I dig into my pocket and pull out the black box. I flip open the lid, revealing a modest half-carat solitaire diamond ring. "I bet you won't marry me and make me the happiest man alive?"

Tears fill the corner of her eyes as she looks between the ring and my hopeful smile before putting me out of my misery. "That's a bet I will gladly take." Her arms wrap around my neck while she presses her lips to mine. When she pulls away, she holds out her hand as I pull the white gold band from the box and place it on the ring finger of her left hand. "Also, I win."

The End

Read Bennett's story in Flirting with the Playboy.

Flirting with the sexy stranger on a dating app was easy.
Finding out the sexy stranger is also the office playboy...
I wasn't expecting that.

They don't call Bennett Pierce the office playboy for nothing. The parade of women through his doorway makes me want to dry-heave. Sure, he looks as if he strolled off the page of a male fashion magazine, but his personality is anything but desirable.

But after catching my ex cheating on a dating app and Bennett witnessing my very public break up, his offer of margaritas is too hard to pass up. Tequila didn't make my clothes fall off, but it did lead to one scorching hot kiss.

Instantly, I regret it but an unexpected message on the dating app distracts me from too much self-loathing. And when the friendly banter quickly turns into steamy flirting, Bennett Pierce is one swipe right forgotten.

And when we finally meet, I realize...
I've been flirting with the playboy.

Flirting with the Playboy
Available Now

acknowledgments

First and foremost, I want to thank everyone who picked up this book. I think I will forever be in awe that someone wants to read my stories.

I have to thank my husband. I don't know if I would have ever started writing and publishing journey without his words of encouragement. A big shout out to Brandi Zelenka. You were there for me every step of the way and I don't think I could have done this without you.

To my creative team, you pushed me to put out the best book possible and I am so thankful to have you on my side. Thank you to my editor, Brandi at My Notes in the Margin. I tend to give you a hot mess and you make it brilliant. Thank you so my beta readers, Ashley Cestra and Breanna Harkins. You gave me invaluable feedback to help make my manuscript sparkle. And my proofreader, Jo at Illuminate Author Services, your eye for catching those pesky errors that squeaked by is amazing. Jessica Hollyfield and Kristi Webster, you both are fantastic cheerleaders and I am so honored to have you both in my corner and answer all my oddball questions.

I hope to see you at the next book!

other titles by
Gia Stevens

about the author

Gia Stevens resides in the *up north* of Minnesota. She lives for the warm, sunny days of summer and dreads the bitter cold of winter. A romantic comedy junkie at heart, she knew she wanted her own stories to encompass those same feelings.

When she's not busy writing your next book boyfriend, Gia can be found playing in her vegetable garden, watching re-runs of The OC and Gossip Girl, or curled up with a good book.

Visit my website for more information.

Printed in Great Britain
by Amazon

28744550R00040